MY FIVE SENSES

Hearing

Published by Smart Apple Media, 1980 Lookout Drive, North Mankato, Minnesota 56003.
Copyright © 2004 Smart Apple Media. International copyrights reserved in all countries.
No part of this book may be reproduced in any form without written permission from the publisher.
Printed in the United States of America

PHOTOGRAPHS BY Corbis, Richard Cummins, Tom Myers, Photo Researchers, Inc. (Peter Cull/Science Photo Library),
Bonnie Sue Rauch, Tom Stack & Associates (Joe McDonald, Brian Parker, Wm L. Wantland), Unicorn Stock Photos
(Eric R. Berndt, Jeff Greenberg/MR, James A. Hays, Paul A. Hein, Gary Randall)
DESIGN Evansday Design

Library of Congress Cataloging-in-Publication Data
Hidalgo, Maria.
Hearing / by Maria Hidalgo.
p. cm. — (My five senses)
Summary: Briefly describes the parts of our ears and how they enable us to hear sounds.
Includes bibliographical references and index.
ISBN 1-58340-304-3
1. Hearing—Juvenile literature. [1. Hearing. 2. Ear. 3. Senses and sensation.] I. Title. II. My five senses (North Mankato, Minn.)
QP462.2 .H53 2003
612.8′5—dc21   2002030907
First Edition
2 4 6 8 9 7 5 3 1

MY FIVE SENSES

Hearing

MARIA HIDALGO

4

YOUR SENSES HELP YOU LEARN

ABOUT THE WORLD AROUND YOU.

There are 5 senses:

SMELL

SIGHT

TASTE

TOUCH

HEARING.

You hear with your ears.

Ears can hear many different things.

They can hear

WHISPERS
AND THUNDER.

A SINGING BIRD
AND A LAUGHING FRIEND.

ALARM CLOCKS,
SIRENS,
AND AIRPLANES IN THE SKY.

Bats "see" in the dark by making noises and listening for the echoes they make.

Hearing helps you **communicate** with other people.

It can also keep you safe.

When you cross a street, you use your eyes and your ears.

You look to see if a car is coming.

But you also listen.

You can hear a car before you can see it.

8

A BIRD SINGS.

9

A HORN HONKS. A DOOR SLAMS.

You may not pay attention
to all the sounds around you.

But your ears hear
every sound.

If you could see sounds,
they would look like water waves.

These waves move through
the air to your ears.

The shape of your ears
helps you catch the waves.

A baby knows the sound of his mother's voice right after he is born.

Inside your ears,
sound waves turn into messages.

These messages are sent
to your brain.

Your brain **ignores** sounds
you do not need.

But it lets you hear important things,
such as your mother
calling your name.

12

PEOPLE WHO CANNOT HEAR

SUTPHEN

ST. LOUIS

H&L 6

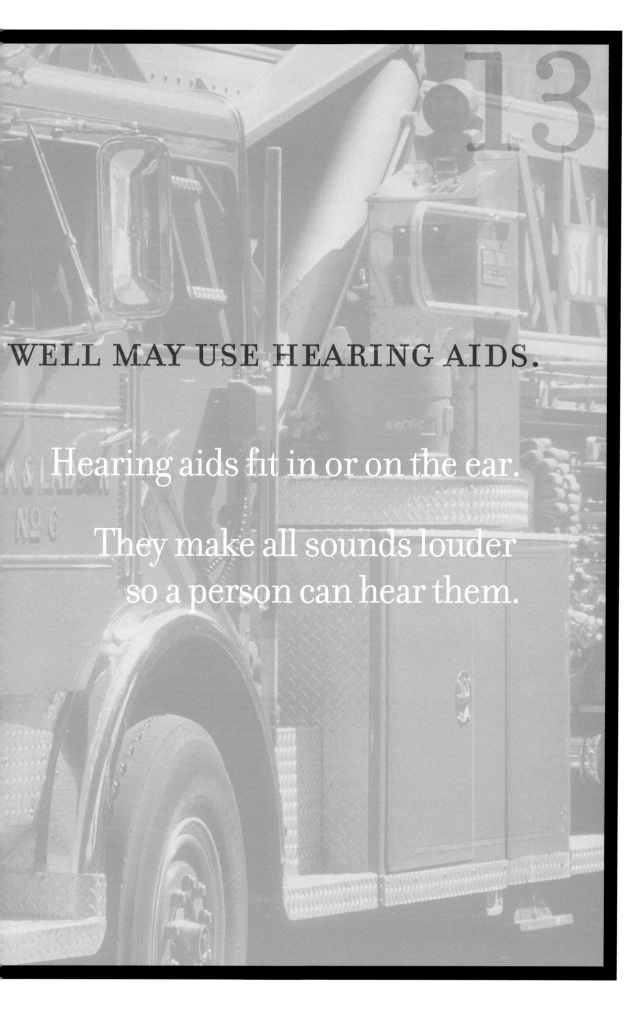

WELL MAY USE HEARING AIDS.

Hearing aids fit in or on the ear.

They make all sounds louder
so a person can hear them.

People who cannot hear at all
can still communicate.

Many **deaf** people learn to read lips.

They watch people's mouths and
figure out what they are saying.

Sign language lets deaf people
communicate with their hands.

Your ears help you hear sounds. But they
also help you keep your balance.

Some deaf people have special TVs that change sounds and voices into words.

Some special doorbells have lights that flash when they ring.

And hearing dogs are trained to tell their deaf friends about important sounds.

To feel how sound waves feel to your ears, touch a drum while it is being played.

16

YOUR EARS MAKE EARWAX

TO KEEP THEM SAFE.

Earwax is sticky.

It catches dirt before it gets
deep inside your ears.

Once the earwax has dirt in it,
it dries up and falls out.

Do not put anything in your ears.

You could push earwax
too deep into your ears.

Or you could plug your ears.

This could hurt your ears
and your sense of hearing.

Sounds are measured in decibels. Whispers measure
30 decibels. Space shuttles measure 120 decibels.

You also should not listen to too many loud noises.

This can hurt your hearing, too.

So keep your TV and radio turned down.

You have so many other things to hear and enjoy!

Deaf people can call hearing people on special telephones. They type what they want to say.

20

communicate to tell people things and to understand what they are telling you

deaf unable to hear

ignores does not pay attention to

senses things that let you see, smell, taste, hear, and touch the world around you

Sound Feelings

Kids who are deaf cannot hear, so they learn to talk by feeling sounds.

WHAT YOU NEED

A friend

A balloon

WHAT YOU DO

1. Blow up the balloon.

2. Face your friend and hold the balloon between your mouths.

3. Have your friend say your name into the balloon. Use your lips to feel the balloon. How does the feeling change as he says the different sounds in your name?

4. Put your hands over your ears. Now, have your friend say letters from the alphabet into the balloon. Can you tell what he is saying?

Read More

Cole, Joanna. *Magic School Bus Explores the Senses.*
New York: Scholastic, 2001.

Hurwitz, Sue. *Hearing*. Danbury, Conn.: Franklin Watts, 1999.

Molter, Carey. *Sense of Hearing*. Edina, Minn.:
Abdo Publishing Company, 2002.

Explore the Web

KIDSHEALTH

http://kidshealth.org/kid

NEUROSCIENCE FOR KIDS: THE SENSES

http://faculty.washington.edu/chudler/chsense.html

THINKQUEST: COME TO YOUR SENSES

http://tqjunior.thinkquest.org/3750